VILLAGE

In the forest
on the far side
of the village
there lived a
pack of wolves.

FOREST

The villagers warned their children **never** to go
into the forest on their own, and to yell out
if they **ever** saw a wolf approaching.

words by **James O'Neill**    pictures by **Russell Ayto**

PICTURE CORGI

UK | USA | Canada | Ireland | Australia
India | New Zealand | South Africa

Picture Corgi is part of the Penguin Random House
group of companies whose addresses can be found
at global.penguinrandomhouse.com.

www.penguin.co.uk
www.puffin.co.uk
www.ladybird.co.uk

Penguin
Random House
UK

First published 2016
001

Text copyright © James O'Neill, 2016
Illustrations copyright © Russell Ayto, 2016
The moral right of the author and illustrator
has been asserted

Printed in China
A CIP catalogue record for this book
is available from the British Library

ISBN: 978–0–552–56845–6

All correspondence to:
Picture Corgi
Penguin Random House Children's
80 Strand, London WC2R 0RL

MIX
Paper from
responsible sources
FSC® C018179
www.fsc.org

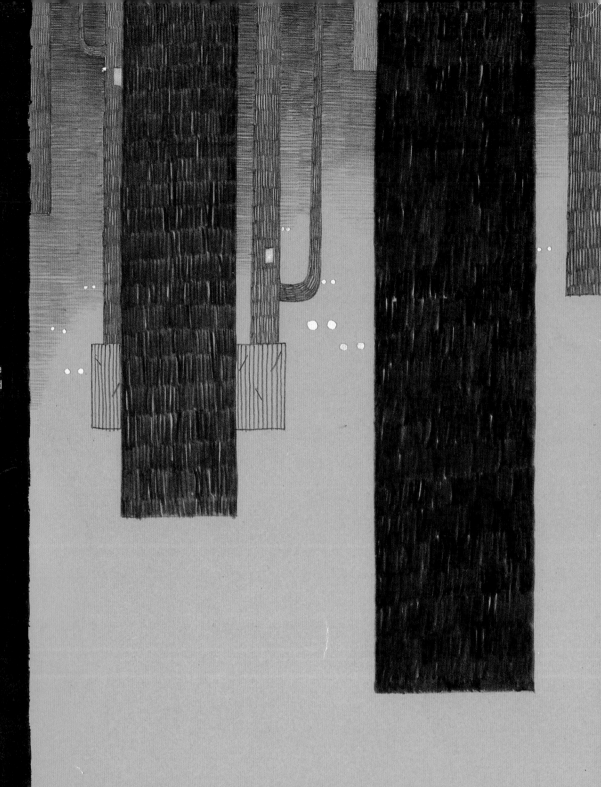

And for good reason –

DANGER!

# wolves are dangerous animals!

(You see, sometimes your parents are right.)

But as it happens,
these wolves
weren't dangerous.

(You see, sometimes
your parents are wrong.)

In fact, not only
were these wolves
not dangerous,
they weren't
even scary.

They were
soft,

they were
playful,

they were the friendliest wolves
you could ever meet.

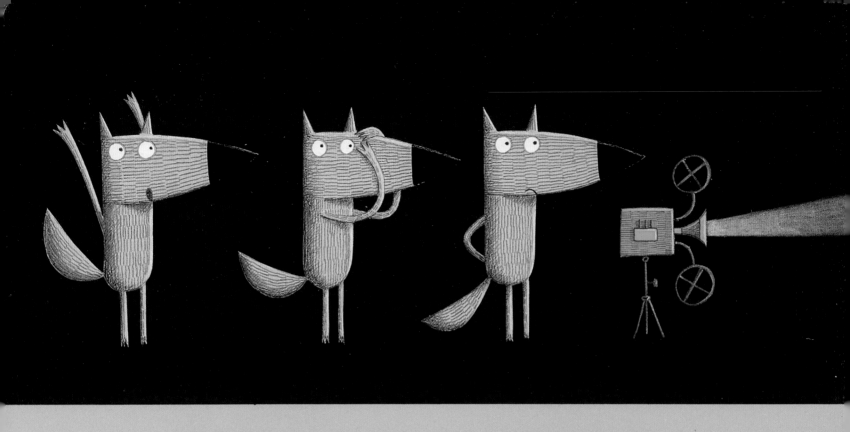

Now, all the wolves of the forest warned their cubs
to stay away from the village, and to let out a big roar
if they **ever** saw a villager approaching.

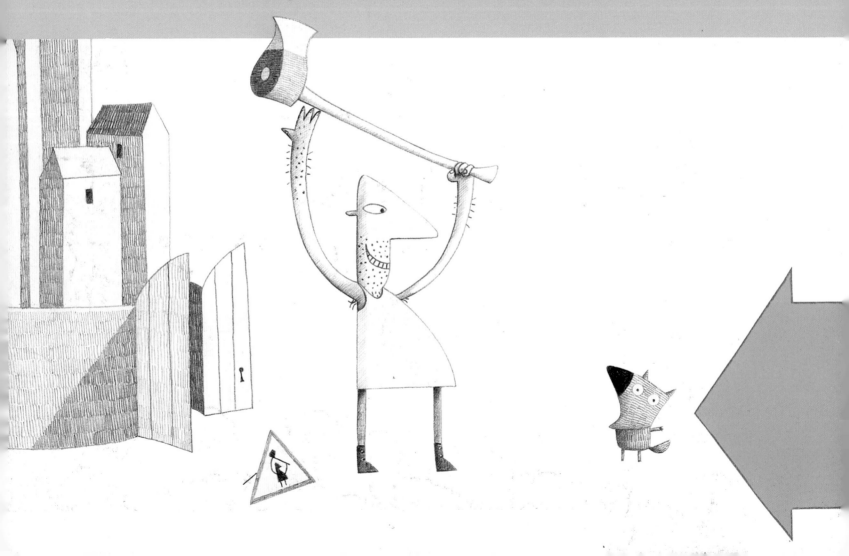

And for good reason –

the **villagers**
**didn't** like
the **wolves!**

DANGER!

DANGER!

Every wolf knew that!

But one little wolf cub knew it better than anyone.

This little wolf thought he was brave . . .

but
he
wasn't.

He thought he was strong . . .

but
he
wasn't.

He thought he was ferocious . . .

but he really,
**really** wasn't.

This little wolf was always scared the wolves were about to be attacked.

Sometimes he yelped, "Help!"

Sometimes he howled, "Over here!"

But most of all he cried, "Boy!"

He cried, "Boy!" whenever shadows suddenly fell across the trees.

He cried, "Boy!" whenever there was a rustle in the undergrowth (usually a terrified mouse).

He cried, "Boy!" whenever the wind tickled his ears as he was dozing off to sleep.

He was always crying, "Boy!"

To begin with, the entire pack would come racing to the rescue.

But now – because there never ever was a boy when they got there –

none of them really bothered much . . .

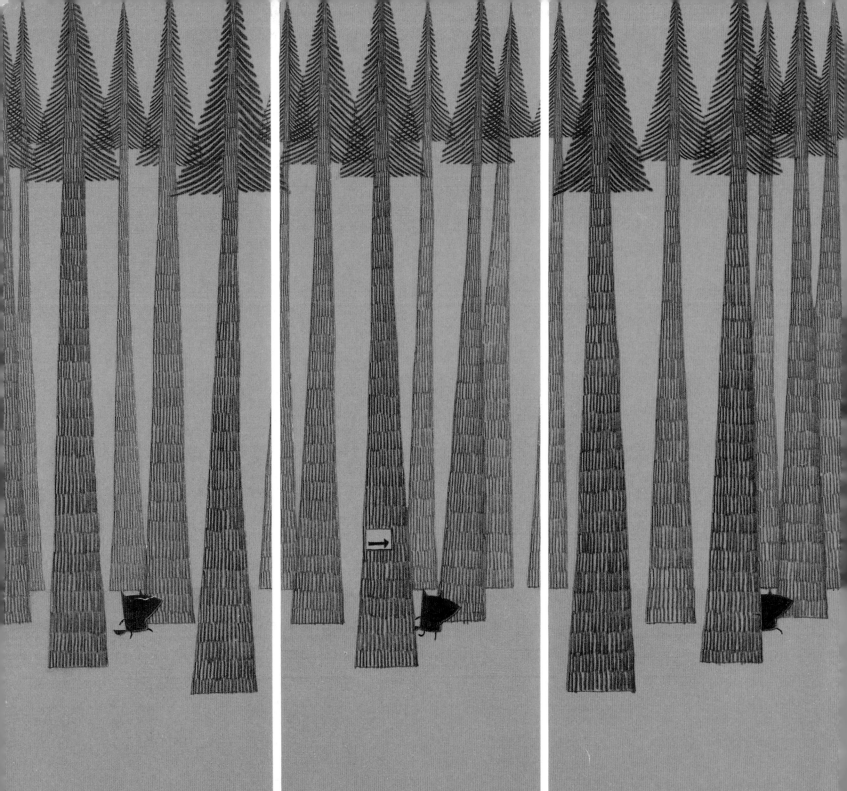

One unusually warm spring morning, the little wolf decided to go to the stream to cool off.

The stream was a little bit near the wood, but also a little bit near the village.

But the sun was so strong that all he could think about was jumping into the cool, fresh water.

Just as he passed the last trees of the forest, the little wolf spied something.

He crept forward to get a better look . . .

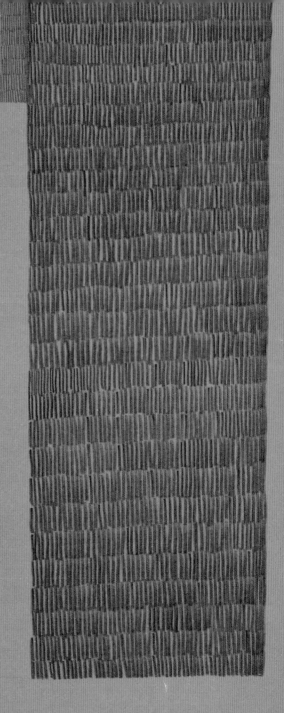

Two arms?
Yes.
Two legs?
Yes.
Scruffy T-shirt and shorts?
Yes.
Face smeared with chocolate, jam and juice?
Yes.

There was
no doubt about it . . .

# That was a boy.

VILLAGE

But not just any boy.

This little boy thought he was brave . . .

but
he
wasn't.

but
he
wasn't.

He thought he was strong . . .

He thought he was ferocious . . .

but he really,
**really** wasn't.

This little boy was always scared the village was about to be attacked.

Sometimes he yelled, "Danger!"

Sometimes he hollered, "Come quick!"

But most of all he cried, "Wolf!"

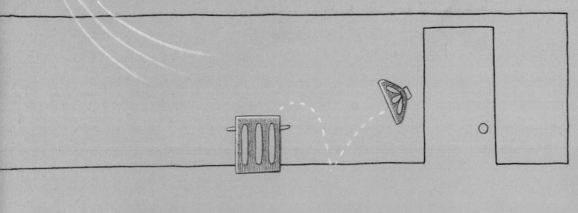

He cried, "Wolf!" whenever the lid
was blown off the bin in the yard.

He cried, "Wolf!"
whenever a cow
went MOO!

He cried, "Wolf!" whenever
the wind tickled his ears as
he was dozing off to sleep.

This little boy was always crying, "Wolf!"

**And yes, you've guessed it** (well, you've probably heard of him before, haven't you?),

there was never a wolf to be seen . . .

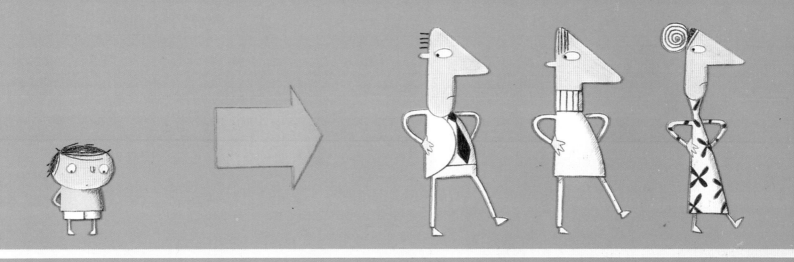

And all the villagers had long grown tired of responding to his calls.

So, what do you think happened when the little wolf and the little boy met? Well . . .

they both let rip!

BOY!

BOY!

BOY!

WOLF!

WOLF!

WOLF!

WOLF!

This went on for some time . . .

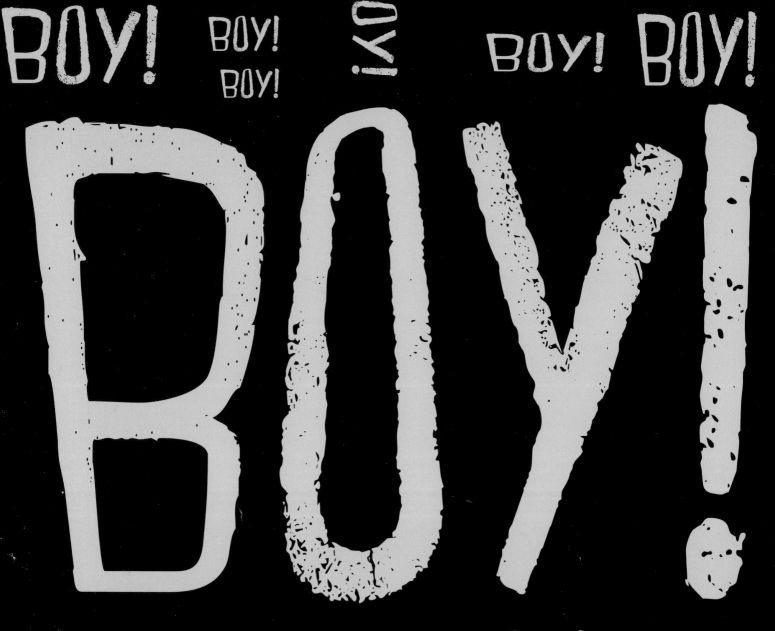

But not one villager raised a head, and not one wolf cocked an ear.
They'd heard it all before.

Now, screaming and howling is tiring work –
especially when you're only a little wolf and a little boy.
Before long they decided to stop for a break.

They were tired, they were thirsty.
The water looked so cool and fresh . . .

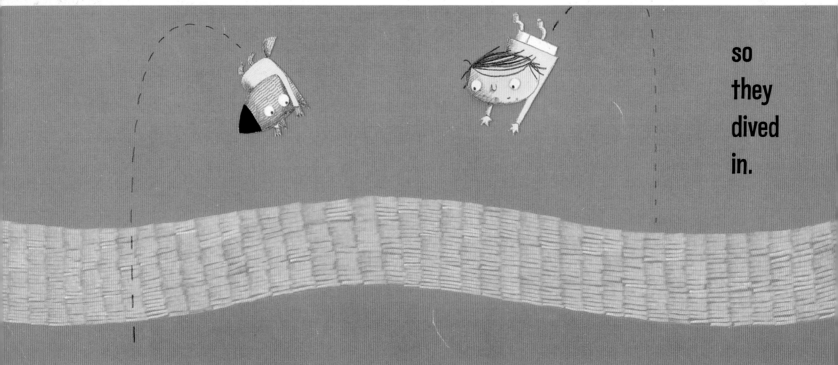

so
they
dived
in.

They jumped,
they splashed,
they paddled,
they danced.

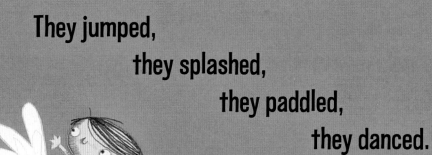

The little boy leapt on
the little wolf's back.

The little wolf leapt
on the little boy's.

They raced, they chased,
they played,
they lazed.

And in this way
a long afternoon passed until . . .
who should turn up?

and the villagers looked at the wolves,

and then they all looked at the little wolf and the little boy.
It looked as if their fun was over.

The little wolf and the little boy felt both happy and sad.
Happy, because of the wonderful time they had spent together.

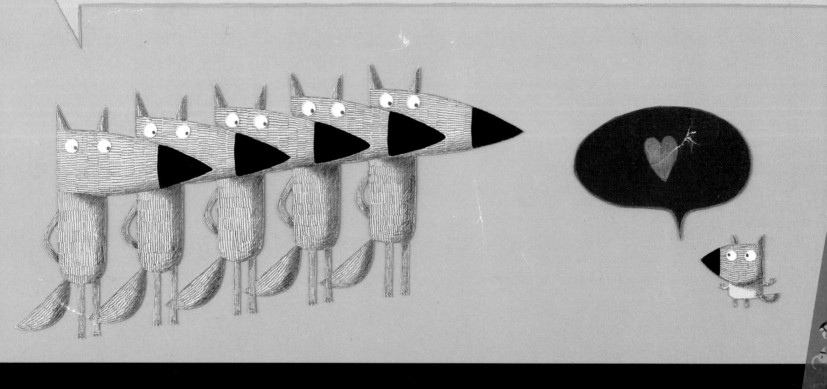

sad, because it didn't look as though they would ever be allowed to play together again. (You see, not all stories have a happy ending.)

But with a little more courage and a little less fear . . .

. . . sometimes
they do.